The Judge

An untrue tale by
Harve Zemach:

The Judge

With pictures by
Margot Zemach

Farrar, Straus and Giroux

New York

For David and Shanna

This is prisoner number one.
Let justice be done!

Please let me go, Judge.
I didn't know, Judge,
That what I did was against the law.
I just said what I saw.

A horrible thing is coming this way,
Creeping closer day by day.
  Its eyes are scary
  Its tail is hairy
I tell you, Judge, we all better pray!

The man has told an untrue tale.
Throw him in jail!

This is prisoner number two.
What did he do?

Please let me go, Judge.
I didn't know, Judge,
That what I did was against the law.
I just said what I saw.

A horrible thing is coming this way,
Creeping closer day by day.
   Its eyes are scary
   Its tail is hairy
   Its paws have claws
   It snaps its jaws
I tell you, Judge, we all better pray!

There must be something wrong with his brains.
Put him in chains!

This is prisoner number three.
A scoundrel, I see.

Please let me go, Judge.
I didn't know, Judge,
That what I did was against the law.
I just said what I saw.

A horrible thing is coming this way,
Creeping closer day by day.
  Its eyes are scary
  Its tail is hairy
  Its paws have claws
  It snaps its jaws
  It growls, it groans
  It chews up stones
I tell you, Judge, we all better pray!

Lock him up and throw away the key.
He can't fool me!

This is prisoner number four.
Have I seen her before?

Please let me go, Judge.
I didn't know, Judge,
That what I did was against the law.
I just said what I saw.

A horrible thing is coming this way,
Creeping closer day by day.

Its eyes are scary
Its tail is hairy
Its paws have claws
It snaps its jaws
It growls, it groans
It chews up stones
It spreads its wings
And does bad things
I tell you, Judge, we all better pray!

Take that nincompoop out of my sight.
Lock her up tight!

This one is the fifth and last.
He'd better talk fast.

Please let me go, Judge.
I didn't know, Judge,
That what I did was against the law.
I just said what I saw.

A horrible thing is coming this way,
Creeping closer day by day.

Its eyes are scary
Its tail is hairy
Its paws have claws
It snaps its jaws
It growls, it groans
It chews up stones
It spreads its wings
And does bad things
It belches flame
It has no name
I tell you, Judge, we all better pray!

Liar! Ninnyhammer! Dimwit! Dunce!
To jail at once!

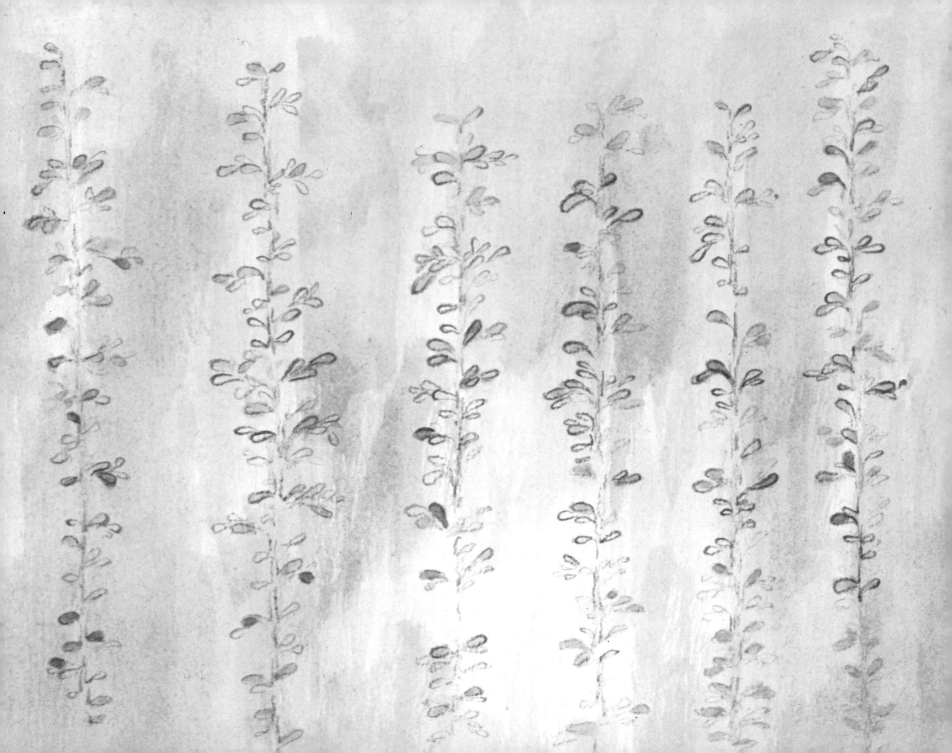